Plenty Of Freaks Are You Sold On Online Dating?

SIDNEY S. PRASAD

ISBN-10:1927676266
ISBN-13:978-1-927676-26-4

DEDICATION

I dedicate this book to my good friend Lucky who encouraged me to write about my raunchy dating adventures. Lucky you are a strong woman and I applaud you for attracting your soul mate without having to resort to online dating!

CONTENTS

ACKNOWLEDGMENTS

I'd like to take a moment and congratulate all the men and women who are risk takers and are active in the world of dating. My heart goes out to those people who have had their heart broken while on the quest for love. Most people today are aspiring in finding their one true love. However, that road to success is an uphill ride for some. Life would be easier if there was a user care manual that we could lean on when obstacles arose in the dating scene. Some people reading this book may be self-proclaimed players and veterans to the dating world, while others might be new to the scene. One thing that both people have in common is that they are playing the same game.

Today we live in a fast paced society ranging from fast food to speedy repairs. Everyone seems to want everything delivered yesterday, figuratively speaking. As internet technology advanced, almost the last two decades have focused on online dating. This serves as a fast way of meeting people and falling in and out of love. With dating and technology combined together to quench man's hunger for love results in people having both dates from heaven and hell. I've had the opportunity to be active in the dating field for almost 25 years and have met Plenty of Freaks along the journey. There were times when it was love at first sight. There were other times when I was looking for the exit sign within the first two minutes of the date. After entertaining people with both hilarious and horrific stories, I have always been urged to write a manuscript about my experiences. Prepare to be amused by the stories about the Plenty of Freaks that I have dated.

1 BLIND DATE

Today in the 21st century, we struggle to answer text messages and reply to all of our emails. Plus, we are burdened with the daily commute combined with our personal obligations. With that in mind we are also craving to find that special someone to make our life complete. But who has the time to go out and mingle during this chaotic era that we live in.

The beauty about meeting people via internet is that you get a great vibe of the other person without investing a bunch of time into it. It's not rocket science to discover if your personality resonates with the person that you are chatting with online. With that in mind, most people would agree that the ultimate goal of online dating is to eventually meet in person. This way, you can both decipher if there is mutual attraction or not. Having stated that now, I can't fathom why people would fail to disclose a legitimate picture of themselves or embellish on the picture that they provided. Because as soon as you meet them, the cat is out of the bag, right?

"Order your date fish and you have fed her for the night. Teach her how to fish and you're not getting laid!"

—Sidney S. Prasad, My Bipolar Manager

Some people have a strange false assumption that if they can make a person fall in love with their virtual personality, the other person will overlook the fact that they lied about their weight or their appearance. Honesty is the best policy and something that society preaches to everyone from a young age. The foundation of a truly remarkable relationship is genuine trust. If you are going to lie about the most obvious thing, then you are going to force the other person to second guess everything that comes out of your mouth. The other person will automatically or eventually throw in the relationship towel.

Back in the late nineties, I had a pretty great routine set up for picking up women. During the weekdays, my friends and I would hit on everything that walked at the local colleges and universities. Then, on Friday and Saturday nights, we would hit the nightclubs. Sundays were reserved for crashing wedding receptions. To add a little spice to our agenda, my friends and I would hang out at the airport every now and then to mack on the arriving tourists. The airport was a great gig because it was close to the hospital. The overworked insomniac nurses wouldn't put up a fight and were really receptive in sharing their phone numbers. Who has the energy to fight off a sex-starved, perverted twenty -three-year-old guy after a twelve hour shift, right?

"I went over for a conjugal visit and we did it prison-style."

Sidney S. Prasad

My friend Nick called me one day and invited me to his house. He had a computer hooked up and an AOL chat room thing going. He explained the mechanics of online chatting and then pitched me on the idea of online dating. I stood my ground and was adamantly against it. I told him that the internet is for creeps, weirdoes, and band camp geeks. Nick then conquered my reluctance by showing me some hot pictures of woman that he was corresponding with. Then he shared his philosophy with me that really impacted my life at that point. Nick told me that internet dating is a win win strategy. Nick went on to say that, during the week, you get to know a couple of hotties online and have a date lined up for Friday night. He said, "Why go to the night- club, where it's a free-for-all and twenty guys competing to dance with the same girl?" That made logical sense to me and got me interested in the world of online dating.

"Do social workers help people make friends?"

—Sidney S. Prasad, Don't Ask Dumb Questions!

I immediately invested into a brand new computer and finally threw out my stone-aged typewriter. The first few weeks in the chat rooms were awesome. I would constantly catch myself smiling and laughing away behind the monitor into all hours of the night. The very first girl who I spoke to online made it into my history books for one of the most bizarre dates. I started chatting with a girl named Shalina Gill. She asked me if I had a picture and I honestly told her I barely knew how to use my computer. I then asked her for a picture and she claimed to be in the same situation, not being too technically savvy. I asked her to describe herself, and she said the following description verbatim: "five feet seven" tall, fair skin, silky black hair, big red lips, and weighed 125 pounds. That painted a pretty sexy picture in my head and I continued to correspond with her for three weeks. Within that time, we upgraded to the telephone and had endless late night conversations.

"I gave my online date a bouquet of flash drives and blank CDs."

Sidney S. Prasad

I propositioned Shalina one day and asked her out on a date. Considering that we live in the same city and there is less than a ten minute drive separating us. She agreed to hooking up but had a completely different agenda. My plan was to either a) go for drink at a classy lounge or b) enjoy a candle lit dinner. She said she would rather sit and talk in her car for the first date. I found this odd and suggested a conversation at a coffee house. She finally convinced me into meeting her at the parking lot of the local college. She said she would pack some snacks and we could partake in a long conversation without having to worry about getting dressed up. I was delighted because I got to hold on to my "buy one, get one free" coffee coupon.

"My Stupid CEO got banned from Las Vegas for shitting on the craps table."

—Sidney S. Prasad, My Stupid CEO

Now here is where it got freaky. Right before the date, Shalina had told me about a last minute stipulation. She said it would be adventurous if both of us had blindfolds on and then unblindfold each other at midnight. Shalina figured this coincided with the whole concept of a blind date. Considering this was my first online date and that I was a naïve, twenty-three-year-old, I went along with it. At 7:00 PM, I got out of my car and put a dress shirt around my head that I used as a blindfold. Then I jumped into a blue Chevy Malibu as she instructed. I went to hug her and I could not get my arms around her. Please keep in mind that I'm almost "six feet two" tall so I have really long arms. The reason why I couldn't hug her properly is because as it turned out, Shalina was almost 350 pounds. This chick totally bamboozled me. Her being a chunky butt wasn't the issue at stake; her lying to me was. In my books, if I catch you in a lie just one time, I have to spend the rest of the relationship seconding-guessing everything that comes out of your mouth.

"When you meet someone virtually and the date is going sour, too bad you can't hit delete or throw them in the recycle bin."

Sidney S. Prasad

A lot of thoughts went racing through my mind because the girl had too much of my personal information. Not only did Shalina have my cell phone number and pager number, she also had my work number and house number. I had to choose my actions carefully as this was going to be a delicate maneuver. I didn't want to upset the con-artist and make her think I was ditching her because she was a big girl. So, I grabbed her and gave her a good, thirty-second long kiss. I even tasted some jelly doughnut on her lips. I guess she couldn't wait for me before diving into the snacks. Then, for the next ten minutes like a broken record, I was like: "Oh my God, oh my God, I can't believe I kissed you on the first date. Oh my God, I broke my personal code of ethics!" I told Shalina that I had to end the date and go home to think about what I did because I was disgusted with myself.

As soon as I got home, I called that asshole Nick who sold me on online dating, and proceeded to give him shit for twenty minutes. Nick responded that shit happens, and to go on to the next girl. I'm like, "Fuck that" and went to a nightclub. There is a God, because ironically, two weeks later, Nick called and told me that he was having kinky phone sex with some chick named Shalina Gill. I'm thinking, "Holy sheep shit! What are the chances?"

"Hollywood claims that the camera adds ten pounds. What is your excuse?"

Sidney S. Prasad

I asked Nick if he had seen a picture of Shalina. Shockingly, he said yes. I told him to start-up his computer and I would be at his place in five minutes. Back in the prehistoric late nineties, it took about five minutes to load up a scanned picture of someone. When I arrived at his house, the picture was downloaded and I confirmed Shalina's identity. Imagine there were two guys sitting at the dinner table side by side. Conceptualize someone hiding behind the two guys with their chin resting on their shoulders, so you only see the face. That's the stunt that Shalina pulled. Nick said that he was addicted to the phone sex, and will ride the virtual wave for a couple more weeks. I had my own personal crying game and wished both of them the best of luck.

"I have always wondered if people who can communicate telepathically ever engage in mind sex."

Sidney S. Prasad

2 TOO GOOD TO BE TRUE

Accumulating a large amount of money doesn't happen overnight, unless you fluke out and win the lottery. Respectively, the same thing could be said about attracting the dream girl or guy. Everything in life takes time and effort on both parties. I had an awesome date planned out one Friday night. I was planning to dine at a classy Italian restaurant, followed by a night of dancing, ending with a romantic walk on the beach. I was psyched all week and then Friday night finally came. I was about to get my dancing shoes on, my date, Kiran called me. She sounded like shit because apparently, Kiran caught the flu that was going around. I told her I understood, and we could reschedule our date for another night. Kiran told me that I was a very sensitive guy and she was very lucky to have attracted me into her life.

Thirty seconds after I hung the phone up, I found myself online shopping for a replacement date. I had to feather through the needy girls who just got dumped and were looking for someone to psycho-analyze their situation. After briefly sending messages back and forth with half a dozen girls, I came across this chick named Sonia. She had a hot picture and an amazing personality. I strongly believe when one door closes, another two open up. Sonia seemed perfect and it was almost like she was a carbon copy of me. It was sort of like me sweeping me off my feet. What a dream come true, I thought to myself.

"I don't drink, smoke or gamble but I am a fucken chronic, pathological liar!"

—Sidney S. Prasad, My Bipolar Manager

While chatting with Sonia on the messenger provided by the dating website, my phone rang. I made the mistake of answering it because it was Kiran, my former sick-with-the-flu date. Kiran needed me to go to the pharmacy and pick up some medicine for her, along with some stuff from the market. Unfortunately, I had to end my conversation with Sonia and step out to take care of Kiran's needs. I forecasted this should take no longer than forty-five minutes.

Between Kiran and a pit stop I made at the nudie bar, I got home three hours later. I was sort of regretting my actions as there would be no way Sonia would still be online. Some other pervert probably scooped her up by now. Anyways, I logged onto the dating website and got greeted by Sonia. Immediately, I told myself not to let this opportunity slip. Sonia and I upgraded to the phone and started talking. Sonia openly admitted that she was guilty of polishing off a bottle of wine during the last three hours while I was away. Evidently, alcohol made her frisky and she wanted me to deliver a bottle of wine and drink it with her in her hot tub ASAP. I was totally down with that that idea.

“Officer, I got robbed by a gold digger.”

Sidney S. Prasad

I looked at the time. It was already around 12:30 AM, so all the major department stores were closed. That meant I wouldn't be able to shower myself with their tester colognes. I bit the bullet and used my roommate's cologne and flipped over my underwear. Now I was ready for Sonia. She gave me an address and told me to ring the bell when I got there. I pulled up to a cul-de-sac which was exactly how she described it and parked next to a red SUV. It was about 1:15 AM when I rung the door bell. Nobody answered, so I ended up ringing it another two times. I was expecting Sonia to answer the door in some sexy lingerie and heels. Holy shit! I almost fainted when the door opened because the person that answered was a middle-aged redneck guy, "six feet six" tall with a shotgun in his hand.

My feet were frozen solid to the door step as I was completely caught off guard. The guy was like, "What the fuck do you want and why did you wake me up?" I apologized and told him that I was looking for a girl named Sonia. Before I knew it I caught myself in a shouting match with this dude and it started getting pretty ugly. We started sparring in the middle of his front yard and then an old lady who I presumed was his wife yelled out the window that she was calling the cops. She instructed the guy to get off of me and come back in the house. I ran to my car and luckily made it out of there.

"I love it how women maintain eye contact throughout dinner and look away when the check comes."

Sidney S. Prasad

As I was driving home, I realized two important things: One, was that I'm not getting laid tonight and the other, was that I left my expensive $7 wine at that redneck's doorstep. Fuck. After that event, I needed a real stiff drink and a shoulder to cry on. It was like 2:00 AM now and nobody would be serving alcohol. Everybody has that one loner friend that they can call anytime of the day or night because that person is waiting for their phone to ring. I called up this guy Jack, and told him I needed someone to talk to. Thankfully, he had a garage full of booze and welcomed me with open arms. As we were sharing a cigar outside and having a vodka seven, I proceeded to tell him my story. Jack interrupted me and said, "Please don't tell me that the girl's name was Sonia." I said, "Are you friggen psychic? How did you know?" Jack asked if the house was located at this certain cul-de-sac. I confirmed and then he explained to me that I was a victim of foul play. Apparently, Sonia was a friend of Jacks and every now and then, after she gets dumped, she gets even by fucking over an innocent guy. Jack continued that Sonia and her friends would go online and find a guy to talk dirty with. Then, she would invite the innocent bystander to her place in the middle of the night, giving the address of one of her cul-de-sac neighbors. Sonia and her girlfriends would watch the aftermath as the guy rang the doorbell in the middle of the night.

"You know you are living in the 21st century when you meet a chick on the internet and she wants the first date to be in an online forum."

Sidney S. Prasad

What Sonia had orchestrated that night was ingeniously slimy and I was completely blown away. Jack told me that she had a couple of different online profiles that she changes on a daily basis. Jack even had Sonia's picture and it was completely different than what she showed me online. Sonia just steals other people's pictures and pretends that it is her. This girl obviously has some serious mental issues and it is not worth my time to get even with her. I guess there is some validity into that old saying, if something seems too good to be true it probably isn't.

"If I ask you to go Dutch, are you going to dump me?"

Sidney S. Prasad

3 KEEP IT IN THE FAMILY

Back in the late nineties, forwarding jokes via email was a big trend. Most people weren't that email-savvy and didn't know how to send blind copies. This resulted in everyone's name and email addresses being exposed on the forwarded messages. My friend Nina would always go out of her way to make people laugh. She would send some love by sharing jokes that she came across online. It was normal to receive up to ten forwarded messages any given day of the week from Nina. I would gladly take the torch and re-forward them to my trash folder.

I designated reading personal emails on company time because when else am I going to find the freaking time to read that shit. One day, I was perusing through my emails and noticed a suspicious email from what appeared to be a female sender. I thought, "What the hell?" In the event there was a virus attached to that email, my company can use their resources to clean up the mess. The email was from this chick named Rani. She claimed that she was a friend of Nina's and saw my name and address on the forwarded messages. Rani told me that we have never been formerly introduced but she has heard some intriguing things about me. Well obviously this chick had great taste, come on now. I was flattered by the gesture and didn't think it was odd the way she approached me.

"Dating is like a job interview because you have to sleep with the other person a few times to figure out who the boss is."

Sidney S. Prasad

Rani and I exchanged phone numbers and chatted for a couple of weeks. At the time, I didn't find it strange that every time I would call Rani, she wouldn't pick up. Within ten minutes, she would always call back. Rani preferred to talk during the days when I had my lunch break. That worked out for me because I really didn't want to eat with the degenerates in my office, because they were always molesting my curry burgers with their eyes. I requested that we exchange pictures and Rani was like, "Just meet me at the mall after work". She suggested to meet at the food court of the mall.

I was totally down with this, because at worst, this date was only going to put me back no more than $20. The beauty of food courts is you get to save your $2 tip and put it towards dessert at the dollar store. Rani made it really easy for me. She told me to look for a tall East Indian female standing in front of Taco Time with a guitar in her hand. She was going to pick up a guitar she had on layaway that day and wanted to kill two birds with one stone. After work, I went to the mall and scoped the food court for a female with that description.

"I love to date and never want the fun to end. Marriage and mirage have the exact same meaning in my books."

Sidney S. Prasad

Sure enough, there was an East Indian female there with a guitar as per Rani's description. My gut instinct told me to act conspicuous and not approach her right away. I went to an Asian Restaurant which was geographically next to Taco Time and ordered a drink. From the corner of my eye, I realized that I recognized Rani. In fact, I knew exactly who she was; she was my second cousin's wife and a mother of three. It all made sense now, as her house of cards came tumbling down. Rani never answered the phone when I called because her husband was around and she would always call back ten minutes later. Rani would always talk to me during my lunch breaks because she was a stay-at-home mom. My second cousin was a real jerk and really abusive. However, it still didn't give her the right to cheat on her husband. It's better to get out of one relationship before starting another.

"Why can't I fuck your friends? Don't you love me?"

Sidney S. Prasad

One thing was certain; Rani and I could never be because she was married to my cousin and a really big bullshitter. I casually walked far enough away out of her eyesight just in case she recognized me. For the next five minutes, I hid in the music store and contemplated on what to do. I could forward the emails to her husband, but then I would be solely responsible for breaking up a marriage. I didn't want that on my conscience, I could call up Nina and tell her to come down and straighten this out. But then my identity would get revealed and this might not work in my favor because I'm dealing with a chronic, pathological liar. All of sudden, I felt this big slap on my shoulders, and I turned around and it was a buddy from my college named Gurjit. He was cool but not the most attractive guy in the world. He was overweight, had a traditional turban, beard, and had a really bad fashion sense. He was wearing shiny dress pants, with two cell phones clipped on his studded belt, accompanied by some K Mart brand high- tops, a flowery silk shirt and a big dangling gold chain against his hairy chest. Gurjit was a real trooper because he accepted the $10 that I paid him to impersonate me. I gave my cell phone and I.D. and walked him to the food court. Let's just say that date lasted less than five minutes.

When I look back at this experience, maybe I should have taken Rani up on her offer and exchanged pictures when I had the opportunity. I would have been ten dollars richer today. But at the same time knowing how she operates, Rani would probably be desperate to find some dirt on me. So I guess my exit strategy was the only way out of this situation.

"The best way to break up with a gold digger is tell her that you are on welfare."

Sidney S. Prasad

4 DIRTY GIRL

While perusing through the local available cupcakes for my flavor of the week, I came across a picture of an attractive female who had long curly black hair, and no visible moles or facial hair. According to Amrita's profile, she was divorced with a kid. I'm thinking, "Perfect! The kid will keep her distracted half of the time and I won't have to worry about another needy East Indian girlfriend". You see the beauty of dating a single mom is that their number one priority is usually their kids. So basically, they won't have time to monitor my last log in on the dating websites. Plus, it gives me some time to work on a couple of more booty calls.

We started exchanging messages and I nonchalantly asked her about her living arrangements. She told me that her son goes to his father's house on the weekends. I thought to myself, while the kid is playing with his daddy, I can play with his mommy. I arranged a date for Friday night and we met at a lounge. In person, Amrita was even more attractive and she didn't smell like a spice rack which was a huge bonus. We enjoyed a glass of wine and totally hit it off. After the date I walked her to her car. When I opened her door, I was amazed. The inside of her car was filthy as I could not see her floor that was camouflaged by fast food wrappers and garbage. When I kissed her good night, I caught a glimpse of the buildup of dust on her dashboard.

"Online dating is like a video game except you get to sleep with the freaks on the screen."

Sidney S. Prasad

With respects to safety, I always get all my late night dates to call me when they get home. Obediently, Amrita did call and thanked me for a great time. Amrita then invited me for dinner at her place for Saturday night. She told me that after dinner, we could get drunk and have a movie marathon. Amrita also invited me to crash at her place because she knew how I felt about drinking and driving. I gladly accepted her invitation and went to sleep.

The next day, I got all spiffed up and wore some loose jeans for easy access and a dress shirt with snap on buttons. This would make it easier in the event Amrita wanted to rip the shirt off my body. Like clockwork, I stopped by the mall and sprayed on some free cologne testers. When the cologne counter clerk wasn't looking, I sprayed my crotch a couple of times. My next stop was the hospital intensive care unit where I borrowed a bouquet of flowers. When I arrived at her house, Amrita greeted me with a tight hug and big sloppy kiss.

"Did you ever wonder why unemployed people and welfare recipients never get to be contestants on game shows? Because they could really use the fucken money!"

—Sidney S. Prasad, My Bipolar Manager

The night before, I should have realized that her messy car was a red flag. When I stepped into her house I thought she got robbed or something. To start off, every couch in the family room had stuff on it ranging from makeup, books and boxes. As we entered the kitchen, the entire kitchen table was covered with open boxes of cereal, soup cans and pretty much all the contents of a typical pantry. To top it off, her sink was overflowing with dishes and the kitchen counters were covered with dirty pots. I questioned Amrita if she just moved in. Amrita laughed and said she has been really busy and hasn't had time to clean. I'm a busy sales executive but still schedule time to change my underwear I thought to myself. Amrita said not to worry as we could eat in the den.

"Too bad antivirus software can't get rid of the herpes my online date gave me."

Sidney S. Prasad

It's no secret that I am the biggest germaphobe on the planet. I knew I had to get out of this freak's house within ten minutes maximum or I was going to die. I asked Amrita if I could use the shitter and strategize an escape plan. As I went upstairs, I noticed the washer and dryer had clothes pouring out of it, which created a big pile of clothes on the floor. I walked through the hallway and peeked into the bedrooms, discovering that both of the bedrooms floors were littered with clothes and all kinds of funky shit. This reinforced that Amrita and I can never get together because she was a slob.

When I got to the washroom, I opened the medicine cabinet and confirmed she had aspirin in it. Then I exercised my special ability and shit on demand. Instead of flushing the toilet paper that I wiped my hairy ass with, I purposely threw it in the garbage. I then went downstairs and asked Amrita if she had some aspirin. She went up to the washroom and screamed, and I assumed it was because of her shitty discovery in the garbage. Amrita came downstairs and threw the aspirins at me, telling me to get out and never call her again. The only question I am plagued with is how long she waited until she threw the garbage away.

"Positive thinking doesn't work when you're about to shit your pants."

—Sidney S. Prasad, My Bipolar Manager

5 SHE'S GOT LEGS

With all the drama that I encountered with the mainstream chat rooms, I thought I would go back to my roots and test out an East Indian dating website. The concept was quite similar with detailed profiles, picture options and an instant messenger. I was surprised by how many local females from my area had their profiles listed. While searching for the flavor of the week one day, I received an instant chat message from this dame named Reena. While I was chatting with her, I checked out her profile that stated she was "five feet five" tall and a psych nurse. Everyone has their own special body part that they are attracted to on the opposite sex and for me, it's legs. I usually prefer to date taller females just on that basis.

Reena was extremely persuasive and I almost wished that she worked for me because she would have made a fabulous saleswoman. You figured I would have learned my lesson by now, but I'm a man with animalistic needs. Reena convinced me to pick her up that night and go to the movies with her. Based on her persistence and confidence, I gave her a chance. When I arrived in front of Reena's building, a woman that was about "five feet one" tall came out and gave me a big hug. I was pissed off, but before I could give her shit for being short, she told me that she was "five feet five" tall with heels and jumped into my car. I thought, "Fuck it." Now I'm stuck because she is in my car.

"Karma is a bitch! I'm curious on what I did in my last relationship to be punished dining with this bitch?"

Sidney S. Prasad

I have nothing against anyone who is short, tall, fat or slim. However, I don't think it's cool to initially lie, especially about the most obvious thing. A lot of my female friends have reported running into the exact same scenario with guys embellishing their heights. The majority of the female victims ended the date immediately or the relationship was short lived on the merit of that lie. A lot of the notorious bullshit artists on the internet think there is a sucker out there who will view their lie as a minor oversight. It sickens me to think how someone can lie without remorse. Especially when they know they will be busted on the first date. I should have seen this as a red flag but continued with the date.

We proceeded to the movie theatre and couldn't agree on a movie. By the time we agreed on a movie, everything was playing. I suggested to Reena that we hit a lounge and have some appetizers, and come back for the late show. Reena appeared to be normal during the course of our conversation at the lounge and I didn't detect a little freak inside of her. I looked at my watch and mentioned that we should leave for the movie. She then suggested to rent a DVD and watch it at her place. I didn't think much of it and was down with saving my prepaid cinema gift card for a potential future taller girl.

"I think the word date is an abbreviation for Dangerous, Amusing Terrifying, Event."

Sidney S. Prasad

Reena caught me off guard when she asked me a profane question as she stuck the DVD into the DVD player. She asked me where I prefer to have our wedding reception, Grand Taj Banquet Hall or Riverside Banquet Hall? There was no sarcasm in her voice and she was dead serious. I danced around the question without giving her a direct answer. I told Reena that I was a fan of the ambience at the Grand Taj Banquet Hall. As the movie started, she continued with questions related to our future kids and white-picket-fence house. I was really creeped out and wanted to put her on a rocket ship and send her back to planet Bizarro. Most people at that point would have ran for the door. I promised myself not to touch this girl but just finish the movie and bail. I knew any sudden movement might have a negative stimulus on this nut job. When the movie ended, I gave her a quick hug and went to my girlfriend's house.

There's a huge debate on giving closure to the party getting dumped. One school of thought enforces informing the person that things aren't working out and that they are not interested in going further. Then there is the easy way which is to ignore the emails, text messages and phone calls until the person gets the hint. When dealing with a psycho, I prefer just to cut the person out completely, pull a Houdini and disappear. During the next five weeks, Reena left me some fucked up messages at work such as: "Don't you love me anymore?" or "I thought we were an item?" I explained the situation to both of my secretaries and got them to listen to the messages. Both of my colleagues hypothesized that based on Reena being a psych nurse working with people who were mentally challenged, there is a possibility that she might have developed some of the character traits and symptoms of her environment. I was willing to accept that theory and continued to ignore the messages. Finally, after two and a half months, the phone messages from Reena stopped.

"You have a pretty interesting online dating profile; did your psychiatrist help you put it together?"

Sidney S. Prasad

In my mind, Reena was a terrible ambassador to that East Indian dating website so I decided to opt out. Opting in and out of dating websites is pretty normal behavior for people in the online dating world. You go on a couple of disaster dates, meet some psychos and take a breather. Ideally, I never wanted to see Reena for the rest of my natural life. I figured the odds would be in my favor living in a city with a population 3.5 million people. For the next little while, I defaulted back to combing the supermarket for babes and hitting on the occasional protesting teacher that was on strike.

The funny thing was that every time I would make a pass at a random stranger, in conversation later, the girls would tell me that they are on that same East Indian Dating website. Eight months passed since the Reena incident and I figured she was probably locked up by now, or an exhibit at the Zoo. I re-created a profile on the East Indian dating website and got action as soon as I pushed the activate button. Keep in mind that I used exactly the same detailed profile from the previous time. The woman that contacted me was quite adamant that we should meet up for a drink that very same night.

"How do you give crap to someone in sign language?"

—Sidney S. Prasad, Don't Ask Dumb Questions!

I thought there is no harm in cutting to the chase and having an innocent drink with a lonely soul. That night as I drove to the woman's condo, some thoughts started lingering through my mind: A single East Indian psych nurse living in a condo at the exact address of Reena. I truly believe that we talk to God in our prayers and he answers back in our intuition. My gut instinct told me to stand this girl up and chill at the nearby casino which had lots of cameras and armed security. For the next half hour, I received thirteen messages from the girl that I stood up.

"I noticed on your online dating profile under the subject heading: Personality, you put multiple."

—Sidney S. Prasad, My Bipolar Manager

The next day, I was texting one of my friends and accidently answered the phone. Sure enough, Reena ended up being the girl that I stood up. Reena started giving me shit for standing her up and openly admitted that she recognized my profile. Reena told me her intention was a reconciliation to our previous relationship. I responded to her that one date doesn't constitute as a relationship. I also suggested that she should seek some professional help. The next day, I received some psychotic text messages from Reena including death threats. I finally texted Reena and told her that if she doesn't stop, I am going to the Police and pressing charges. Reena's text messages finally stopped.

Once again, I decided to say to hell with that East Indian dating website, and deleted my profile. When I logged in, I found a message in my inbox from the Website Administrator. The email stated that they received a complaint that my profile was made under false pretenses. The Website Administrator requested that in order to keep my membership, I must photocopy my driver's license and fax it to their headquarters in India. I'm thinking that's odd as I've only been on this website for less than 24 hours and have talked to one person. I guess Reena's revenge was to make a phony report and get me booted off the website. Fuck, if anything, she did me a favor and saved me from the other nuts lurking around there. I emailed the website administrator and told them to kill my profile and opt me out.

"Times are changing. In the 60's, the guy with the black leather jacket and Elvis hair would get all the women. In the 21st century, the nerdy guy with the pocket protector and a laptop gets all the chicks online."

Sidney S. Prasad

6 STUCK UP

After carefully analyzing my collection of online horror dates, I came up with a brilliant idea. I decided to check out a dating website that catered to local professionals. I figured the average psycho would have cracked during med school residency or half way through law school. Worst case scenario: If the date never worked out, I could string that girl along and get some free professional advice. It was an ingenious strategy I configured.

I started chatting with this dame named Jasmine who was a principal of a private school. Through the course of our emails and brief phone calls, she seemed decent and date worthy. There was a large distance between us as she lived in the ritzy part of town and I was from the suburbs. Both of us agreed to meet up downtown and carpool to a restaurant. She parked behind my car and requested to drive that night. I had no objections with saving my fuel and having a chauffeur for a couple of hours.

I asked Jasmine if she had a particular restaurant in mind and apparently she didn't. I suggested a new Mexican restaurant down the street. At that moment, Jasmine redeemed herself and showed me her true colors. Jasmine basically said that her taste buds were too good for Mexican food. She then made a distasteful comment that Mexican food was like street food. I took great offence to that comment as I love Mexican food. I sometimes fly to California just for the Latin cuisine.

"Internet dating is legalized prostitution and the red light district is your computer."

Sidney S. Prasad

Jasmine said she preferred to check out an East Indian restaurant instead. I had no problem accommodating her request but suggested we go to the East end of town. Jasmine was dead set on this one particular restaurant close by and I went along with it. As she was driving, she had the nerve to ask me how much money I make and the balance of my bank account. No one has ever asked me that question (other than my parents and all my noisy East Indian relatives) and I was blown away. Jasmine continued to ask some more personal questions and I knew that I wouldn't be able to last through dinner with this gold digger.

I needed to escape from this money hungry chick so I pulled a dumb card on her. When we arrived to the restaurant, I observed her putting money into the parking meter. I told her that I thought parking was free at night. She thought I was stupid and drove me back to my car to pay the parking meter. Jasmine was parked three cars behind me and I hopped into the passenger side of my sports car. I slowly jumped over to the driver's side and started my car and then drove away. I was laughing as I was driving and Jasmine chased me for a good twenty miles before giving up. I guess she got the hint because I never heard from her again.

"My Porsche is in the shop. This jalopy is my courtesy car for the next 20 years."

Sidney S. Prasad

7 LONG DISTANCE

It is widely accepted that the relationship goal in life is to attract the mate of one's dreams, fall madly in love and get married. I support the notion of love and finding that one special person. Today, the divorce rate continues to escalate at an alarming figure. I've witnessed firsthand people rushing into marriages where they hardly knew the other person but was infatuated with the idea of love. Dating can be viewed as an interview process and the person who gives the right answers eventually become your heart's apprentice.

Back in the early 2000's, I found myself attracted to this girl named Meena in Toronto, Canada. Her profile displayed a beautiful woman, but what was more attractive was the personality that came with the picture. Meena was a well rounded-woman who also had a business background and shared similar interests as me. We spoke every day for a month and she would even sing me to sleep. Even though we never met, our personalities resonated well together. I could totally conceptualize us meshing as a couple.

"Checking out online dating profiles is just like shopping for a car. It's not hard to spot the Cougars with the high mileage underneath their hoods."

Sidney S. Prasad

Throughout the duration of our conversations, we had those deep, long discussions about life. Meena and I also spoke about hypothetical future situations but agreed that we wouldn't jump into a relationship until we first met. I clearly disclosed that I needed to get a couple of degrees on the wall before getting hot and heavy with anyone. I flew out to Toronto and met Meena. She was a sensational woman and sparks flew immediately for both of us. Meena and I wined and dined and enjoyed each other's company for that brief yet memorable three day trip.

At the end of the weekend, I invited Meena to my city for our next date. I told her that we could rotate visits every month or two. Meena asked me to fly in next month and elope. I thought she was joking but she wasn't. Meena told me that she had a job lined up for me and I could move in with her. This was a shocking proposition for me as I thought we were on the same page of casually dating until I got my degrees on the wall. Meena asked me to meet her parents. She wanted to introduce me as her fiancé. I told Meena that I like her and would like to continue dating her but no shotgun wedding. I then left Toronto and flew back home.

"Does everybody answer the phone when they are having sex?"

—Sidney S. Prasad, Telemarketer's Revenge The Customer Is Always Wrong, Bitch!

On the flight back home, I did some deep thinking and thought what kind of sicko wants to get married after the first date. Meena was a sweet girl who put me in a delicate situation. I genuinely wanted her to find her true love if she was in that place in her life to receive it. I certainly was on a different agenda and had to get out of this relationship. When I got back to town, I called up Meena and thanked her for a lovely weekend. Within the first five minutes, Meena disclosed that we should delete our online dating profiles. I felt highly pressured and didn't realize we were an item.

"Online dating is like a masquerade ball. It's just a matter of time before the makeup and masks come off."

Sidney S. Prasad

This gave me an opportunity to execute an online dating break-up move. Meena was a pretty smart cookie and I'm confident she would test me out in her own ways. I agreed and deleted my profile, but at the same time created a duplicate profile under a different name. An intelligent nut usually double-checks and confirms that another profile wasn't created. Within two hours, I received a voicemail of Meena crying, telling me that it's over and how she knew about the duplicate profile. The break-up move worked and I had no choice in the matter. The sad thing was, if she didn't pull the marriage card out so quickly, I might not have pulled the plug so abruptly.

"Divorcée chat rooms are a lot like buffets because you know that the food has been recycled a couple of times."

Sidney S. Prasad

8 IDENTITY THEFT

Throughout this book, I have emphasized that the entire goal of online dating is to eventually meet your better half. It's always better to disclose your skeletons upfront because it's embarrassing when they accidently come out later on in the relationship. The most common things that women complain that men lie about online are the following: About being married, their height, and their occupation or even having a job. On the contrary, men complain that women online lie about the following: Their weight, their location, and how many people they are dating.

In online dating, you can easily have a smart mate, tall mate, good lover, and of course a rich mate. The quest is to find all those qualities combined into one person. I guess that's why it's not uncommon for people to casually date three or four people at a time. Back in 2006, I had an elaborate arrangement set up with this girl Rekha. She ultimately wanted to be with a guy from the medical field and I wanted to be with a business woman. Both of us would casually date other people but default to each other for sexy time. One Friday, we had made plans to go to the drive-in movies and not watch the movies if you know what I mean.

"Marriage is like getting over a prostitution addiction where you save a lot of money but you don't get to have sex."

Sidney S. Prasad

Prior to the date with Rekha, I made the mistake of checking my inbox for an online dating website. As soon as I signed on, some girl named Sandy instant messaged me. Sandy asked me if I had plans for the night and I told her I wasn't available. Sandy basically told me that she will rock my world if I ditched my plans to meet up with her. I asked Sandy to send me a picture while I mull this over. Holy shit, the picture Sandy sent to me was phenomenal. I did what any typical male would do. I called up Rekha and told her that one of my high-profile clients was in town and needed to see me for an unscheduled meeting, and cancelled our date.

Sandy and I agreed to meet in front of Starbucks and go from there. I took three cold showers and put some ice cubes in my underwear as I was so excited to see Sandy. As I started walking towards the coffee shop, a woman jumped up from her seat. The woman proceeded to run in my direction and gave me a hug. This lady wasn't the utmost attractive; she had major acne and some funky braces. The woman then identified herself as Sandy. I asked Sandy how old the picture was. She apologized and said it was a recent picture of her cousin that she used as bait.

"I forgot to take Viagra and didn't satisfy my online date. I wish I could push Control Alt Delete and retry it again."

Sidney S. Prasad

At that moment, I was really pissed off at her for messing up my guaranteed night of fun with Rekha. In addition, I was disappointed that she fraudulently used someone else's pictures, as I have been victim of this scam too many times. I grabbed Sandy's hands and told her that I think she looks better than her cousin's pictures and glad that we met. I suggested rather than having coffee, to go next door to the lounge and have some drinks and dinner. For the next three hours, we went through a few glasses of wine and sampled a whole bunch of appetizers. I kept a mental tab of how far our bill was accumulating. When the bill finally hit roughly $100, I told Sandy that I had to step outside and call my co-worker Adam to see if he needs a ride in the morning. As soon as I got outside, I ran away laughing.

One hour later, Sandy left me a message with some colorful four letter words. Ethically and spiritually, I am against this sort of behavior of running out on the bill. But I had to stand up for anyone who has ever received a fake picture and wasted their time. My intentions were to teach Sandy a lesson that she would never forgot. I kept her phone message for a good two years and every time I would tell this story to someone, the punch line would be to play the message for them.

"People should be forced to take a lie detector test when creating an online dating profile."

Sidney S. Prasad

9 MOMMY'S GIRL

It's funny how life works as we can never get enough of something that we don't really want. Whenever the topic of online dating comes up, I usually get the same responses from people, where they have admitted to being active on the online dating scene for awhile. After meeting a couple of psychos online, they decide to go back to the old fashion way of meeting people. I have been guilty of skating though both the traditional and nontraditional methods of meeting people.

There was a concert at the local casino one day with a bunch of hip hop artists from the nineties. I viewed this as a great opportunity to meet some women from the same age bracket. Between the intermission and after the concert, I managed to hit on fourteen females. Eleven of them automatically introduced me to their insecure husbands. One of the women ignored me and the other two needed a shower. Since there wasn't anything to go home with, I ended up in front of my computer.

As I was reviewing local events on a social network Meet Up website, I got approached by an interesting woman named Anjali. We chatted online for about an hour and then upgraded ourselves to the telephone. I'm always paranoid about the first phone call to an East Indian woman as I'm scared she might have a funny accent. Don't get me wrong as I'm East Indian myself. But it's hard to get intimate with someone screaming your name that sounds like your mom.

"I understand that you want to break up but I didn't realize we were dating?"

Sidney S. Prasad

Thankfully, Anjali was like me with Desi roots born on western soil. We had an amazing conversation and talked each other's ears off for a solid five hours. The next two weeks, we had some more intense conversations and Anjali seemed really down to earth. She wasn't like the typical East Indian girl that lived with her parents until they got married. Anjali was independent and she had her own place. During the course of our conversations, I made a point of avoiding the hypothetical long term relationship questions and kept it really casual.

It was apparent to me that she wasn't a freak and definitely date-worthy. She agreed to meet me at a lounge for some adult beverages. Before going into the date, I was conceptualizing both of us having a phenomenal night and maybe end up on the dance floor somewhere. When I arrived at the lounge, I alerted the matradee that I was expecting a "five feet eight" tall East Indian female dressed in red.

I have a couple of destinations scoped out that aren't in arms length of my neighborhood designated for online dates. This way, if the girl ends up being hideous or behaves psychotically, my reputation won't be ruined. The other benefit of having some pre-picked dining locations is having the menu prices memorized. In the event my date recommends a restaurant the first thing I do is eyeball the online menu before confirming. The restaurant selection reflects whether the girl is a gold digger or not. Too bad the North American McDonald's didn't serve booze.

"My ex-girlfriend was such a downer. In fact, she got fired from the mental hospital for depressing all the patients."

Sidney S. Prasad

Anyways, a gorgeous tall East Indian woman approached me and confirmed that she was Anjali. I jumped out of my chair and gave her the biggest hug as I was so happy that her picture was legitimate. Out of the corner of my eye, I spotted an old East Indian woman dressed in a sari with a cane. This appeared to be kind of an odd venue for a golden girl to hang out at. Anjali then did something profane that I couldn't personally fathom in a million years. Anjali introduced me to the old bag and said it was her mom. For the next two hours, Anjali, her mom and I sat and conversed at the table.

This was one of the most awkward moments of my life. As I don't even feel comfortable talking to my own parents let alone someone else's. Anjali's mom did a great job of cross examining me and asked the typical brown questions. She wanted to know what my parents did and which year they got off the boat and immigrated to Canada. She was trying really hard to do the mafia thing and trace my blood back to the home country. I confidently answered all of her questions but still couldn't figure out why Anjali brought her mother along.

"A hypocrite is someone who claims that they don't do business on the phone and then calls Pizza Hut to order dinner."

—Sidney S. Prasad, Telemarketer's Revenge The Customer Is Always Wrong, Bitch!

I needed desperately to confront Anjali on what the hell was going on. I had to get rid of her mom briefly in order to say my piece. I remembered Anjali's mom telling me that she was impressed that I was a vegan just like her. But at the same time, she was snacking on a vegetable platter with a ranch dressing dip. This was my golden opportunity to get rid of mommy for a minute. I spoke up and casually mentioned to Anjali's mom that there is egg in most ranch dressing dips. Before she could respond, I flagged a waitress who reinforced that. Anjali's mom immediately went to the washroom to puke or something.

"My Stupid CEO thought a Porsche 911 was a police car."

—Sidney S. Prasad, My Stupid CEO

I asked Anjali why the fuck did she bring her mom because this wasn't Show and Tell. Anjali explained that she thought I was marriage material and wanted to get her mother's blessings. I'd expect this sort of behavior from someone back home desperate to get a Green Card or something. However, Anjali was born and raised in Canada. Anjali then started making plans for our second date that involved meeting my parents. I told her that it's not going to work as I need a woman who cut the umbilical cord a long time ago. I took care of the bill and got the fuck out of the restaurant. At that point, the only sensible thing to do was to go and spend the rest of the evening with my girlfriend.

"I noticed that you deleted me off your Facebook but do you still love me?"

Sidney S. Prasad

10 MUGS AND HUGS

In the great city of Vancouver, there is a monthly East Indian party at a nightclub. More or less, the club is crawling with divorcées desperately seeking their next meal ticket. It is an easy place to get acquainted with easy women. The men that attend that party are even more pathetic but I'll touch on that another time. People at the party always give me a hard time for being in my mid thirties and never have been married yet.

I found myself in my usual routine, sandwiched on the dance floor between two divorcées. The dj started mixing some shitty songs which prompted my dancing partners to go outside for a smoke. When we got outside, they introduced me to another half dozen divorcé chicks and lit up their cigarettes. I have to admit that their friends were pretty hot and I wouldn't mind being their rebound. All of the girls were raving about a new East Indian dating website that they all have their profile listed on. They even made a point of telling me that they recognize half of the girls in the club from that website.

"Since we have established that we are friends with benefits, does that mean you want to share my Medical and Dental as well?"

Sidney S. Prasad

The next morning when I awoke, I realized that I had a divorcée next to me. I guess I must have gotten hammered and ended up with this chick. She was still sleeping so I decided to raid her fridge. I guess this girl was a carnivore because there was nothing that catered to a vegetarian. While I was trying to figure out breakfast, I spotted a computer. Obviously, I was all over that like Paris and Nicole on an Arkansas farm boy. I found that East Indian dating website that the girls recommended the night before and started checking out some profiles.

I was blown away by the goddess-like pictures on the website. Out of nowhere, I felt these arms around me and got greeted by a good morning kiss. Then the woman saw what was on the computer and started savagely swearing at me. She told me to get the fuck out her house and take my shit-stained underwear with me. Talk about insecure, I thought. I have no issues with my girlfriends checking out other guys. At the minimum, this bitch should have given me a cereal bar for the road or something.

Later on that day, I activated myself a profile on that website and started a search. I came across this one profile that really stood out. The content was unbelievable as it really captured my full attention. The personality traits definitely coincided with what I was looking for. However, the woman was only "five feet three" tall and I was a leg kind of guy. I thought maybe it's time to drop my shallowness and look beyond the human form.

"I picked up this chick at the bar last night and we exchanged phone numbers. I called her the next day and pitched her on switching long distance carriers. She seemed kind of surprised at first. I told her she should have asked me what I do for a living when she gave me her number."

—Sidney S. Prasad, Telemarketer's Revenge The Customer Is Always Wrong, Bitch!

I sent an interest to the profile and received a response within a couple of hours. Her name was Shivani and we shared deep intimate conversations over the phone for a week thereafter. I didn't detect anything was wrong with this girl as she seemed decent and upbeat. Both of us were pretty refined and well cultured. We shared the same interests for art galleries, wineries, and live theatre. The picture that Shivani painted in my mind was of an innocent goody-two-shoes.

I scored some free tickets for a play and invited Shivani to join me. Shivani was all for it but she had some prior engagements and couldn't make it. She suggested that I check out the play and meet her for coffee after. That worked out for me as I ended up taking my secretary to the play. Shivani instructed me to meet her at the parking lot of a small strip mall and then we can go into the coffee shop together. For some reason, she claimed that she hates walking into coffee shops alone when meeting a guy. She felt that the other patrons would know it was a blind date. I understood where she was coming from and went along. We already exchanged pictures but Shivani asked me for a description of my vehicle.

"My cheating girlfriend lived in a pretty progressive neighborhood. I would always see naked men jogging from her house."

Sidney S. Prasad

Going into this date, I had no expectations and just wanted to have a casual conversation. Maybe if things went well, we could go on a moonlight walk at the beach afterwards. At 10:05 PM, a beautiful "five feet three" tall female approached my window and introduced herself as Shivani. I can't even begin to tell you what happened next. Shivani asked me if she could come into my car for a moment. So I hit the power locks and let her in. Shivani put a switch blade to my neck and told me to hand over my wallet, remove my gold chain and within a few seconds, a Mustang full of East Indian guys surrounded my car. It was obvious that they were all in cahoots. Shivani opened my wallet and gave me shit for attempting to go out with her with only a $5 bill in there. I explained that I was carrying a couple of green tea bags in my pocket and usually pay a quarter for a cup of hot water. She wasn't amused, but how far can I go on a telemarketer's salary?

"My Stupid CEO thought a serial killer ruined his breakfast."

—Sidney S. Prasad, My Stupid CEO

I guess I shouldn't have put vice president of a publicly traded company on my dating profile. But fuck, which chick would want to go out with a telemarketer? Shivani told me she can't believe she wasted her time on me. She took my license out of my wallet and told me that she knows where I live if I decide to go to the authorities. Within minutes, this terrifying disaster date was finally over. I drove up to the cop station but decided not to pursue an investigation. How the hell am I going to look a Police Officer in the eye and tell him that I just got rolled by a "five feet three" tall female from an East Indian Matrimonial website? I put my faith in the universe and waited for Shivani's next victim to speak up. The bitch took my five dollars and probably paid off her house with it.

"I broke up with my girlfriend at the Opera, because I promised I would leave on a good note."

Sidney S. Prasad

CONCLUSION

Growing up watching American television, I always admired the Great American Dream: Of living next to someone with a hot daughter, becoming best childhood friends, carrying that bond throughout our teen years, later develop to high school sweethearts and get married after prom. Unfortunately, all the chicks on my block looked liked boys growing up and they even drove Big Wheels and owned Tonka trucks. This led me to getting exposed to all of the funky women that I've dated for almost the last two and a half decades.

I have no regrets with all the freaks that I have dated in my life. I truly believe that everything happens for a reason. Some people come into our life for an extended period and stick around for decades. While others may come briefly for a few minutes disguised as waiters or psychotic dates. But we will hold on to their message or lessons that they gave us for eternity. A person could have a couple of divorces under their belt or have dated half the people in the phone book. The only people who lose game are the ones that don't learn from each experience.

Being a career salesman, I have been implanted with the notion that every No gets me that much closer to a buying prospect. Some salesmen close the deal after two rejections while others need to go through one hundred prospects before hitting the gold. Life is essentially a sale where you are selling yourself to a recruiter, attempting to get your foot in the door of the company. You could be selling your friend on the idea of having Italian cuisine tonight rather than Chinese food. Believe it or not, when we are attempting to convince someone to go out with us or vice versa, that can be viewed as a sale as well. The question remains, are you sold on online dating?

The dating saga continues in my next book **Plenty Of Freaks: Worst Online Dating Mistakes.**

ABOUT THE AUTHOR

Sidney S. Prasad is an author on a quest to make the world laugh. His work is focused on entertaining people with his dry-humored novels. Sidney S. Prasad personally believes laughter is the best cure for all of life's ups and downs.

Some other humorous books written by Sidney S. Prasad include:

How To Piss Off A Telemarketer,
How To Piss Off A Salesman
My Bipolar Manager,
My Stupid CEO
Don't Ask Dumb Questions!,
Corny Names & Stupid Places,
Misfortune Cookies,
How To Irritate A Telemarketer
Plenty Of Freaks: Worst Online Dating Mistakes
Plenty Of Freaks: Is Dating Legalized Prostitution?
and
Telemarketer's Revenge: The Customer Is Always Wrong, Bitch!

Made in the USA
San Bernardino, CA
09 April 2014